Star Friends

MYSTIC FOREST

To Eden and Arlo Dawkins – L.C.
To my brother Richard – K.B.

tiger tales

5 River Road, Suite 128, Wilton, CT 06897
Published in the United States 2023
Originally published in Great Britain 2023
by Little Tiger Press Limited
Text copyright © 2023 Linda Chapman
Illustrations copyright © 2023 Kim Barnes
ISBN-13: 978-1-6643-4067-1
ISBN-10: 1-6643-4067-X
Printed in China
STP/3800/0511/0223
2 4 6 8 10 9 7 5 3 1

www.tigertalesbooks.com

Star Friends

MYSTIC FOREST

BY LINDA CHAPMAN

ILLUSTRATED BY KIM BARNES

tiger tales

Contents

Chapter 1
In the Star World
7

Chapter 2
Vacation Time!
12

Chapter 3
Settling In
19

Chapter 4
Shelters and a Scavenger Hunt
43

Chapter 5
Strange Happenings
54

Chapter 6
More Than Just Pranks
69

Chapter 7
Campfire Chaos
80

Chapter 8
Who Could It Be?
89

Chapter 9
Pottery and Pranks
97

Chapter 10
Monkey Mischief
107

Chapter 11
Amazing Violet
123

1
IN THE STAR WORLD

Stardust shimmered and shone on every leaf and every blade of grass, and in a vast forest of tall trees, a wolf, a stag, a badger, and a snowy owl gathered around a sparkling pool. In its mirror-like surface, they could see the image of a coastal town with narrow streets and stone cottages.

"Westport," muttered the wolf, whose fur was tipped with silver. "It has been a few weeks since we checked on our young friends there."

Hunter the owl swept the tip of one wing

over the water. "Reveal the Star Animals and their friends!"

The surface of the pool sparkled even more brightly for a moment and then four different images appeared, each showing a girl and a wild animal with deep indigo eyes.

The stag inclined his majestic antlers toward each pair. "Mia and Bracken," he said, indicating a young fox using his front paws to help an eleven-year-old girl with shoulder-length dark blond hair cram a couple of soft toys and a hoodie into an already full backpack.

"Lexi and Juniper."

He nodded at the red squirrel with bright eyes who was scampering along a curtain rod as a girl with chin-length, dark curly hair packed neatly folded T-shirts carefully into a bag.

"Sita and Willow."

A deer with gentle brown eyes was nuzzling a girl with a long, shiny brown braid who was staring from one heap of jumbled-up clothes to another as if she couldn't decide what to take.

"And Violet and Sorrel."

In the final image, a girl with long strawberry-blond hair tied in a ponytail was pacing anxiously around her bedroom, holding a wildcat with a tabby coat in her arms.

"Our young friends arc going on vacation," said the stag. "Maybe they will now have a chance to use the magic current to help people outside their town of Westport."

The owl nodded, his eyes wise. "Mia, Lexi, Violet, and Sita have learned a lot since they became Star Friends seven months ago."

Every so often, young Star Animals from the Star World traveled to the human world to try and find a Star Friend—a child who believed in magic. When they found a Star Friend, the Star Animal would show that child how to connect with the magical current that ran between the two worlds. Together, the animal and the child would use that magic to do good deeds and to stop anyone who was using dark magic.

The owl began to sweep his silvery wing over the water again to clear the pictures.

"Wait, Hunter!" the badger said suddenly. "Is that another person?"

Looking more closely, the animals all saw that the badger was right. In the center of the pool, a fifth image had formed. The figure was tall and slim, their dark head bent as they kissed the otter snuggled in their arms.

"Well, well, well," said the owl softly. "It appears there is another Star Friend in Westport that I do not believe our young friends know yet." He looked around at the other three animals. "Let us watch and see what happens. This could be very interesting indeed."

2
VACATION TIME!

"All packed!" Mia Greene declared, pulling the drawstring tight on her backpack.

Bracken, her Star Fox, bounced around her, his eyes bright and his bushy tail with its white tip waving from side to side. "We're going on vacation, Mia!"

"This is going to be the best start to Memorial Day weekend ever," Mia said, happiness bubbling inside her. She had been looking forward to this vacation forever—three nights staying at a forest camp with her

best friends, Violet, Lexi, and Sita.

The camp flyer had said that campers would get to do all kinds of forest activities as well as learn outdoor survival skills. When they'd been given the flyer about the camp at school, Mia, Lexi, and Sita had thought it sounded amazing. Violet had taken a little more persuading—she'd never been camping before and wasn't sure she liked the sound of the activities—but she also didn't want to miss out on a vacation with her friends, so she'd asked if she could go, too. Now the day of their trip had finally arrived!

Mia's phone buzzed with a text.

We're here! Vxx

Mia hurried to the window. Violet's dad's large, seven-seater car was outside the house. Sita, Violet, and Lexi were in the back. Seeing her at the window, they waved wildly.

"It's time for me to go!" Mia said to Bracken.

"See you later," said Bracken, licking her nose as she crouched down to give him a hug. "Make sure you call for me as soon as you can!"

"I will!" she promised.

Spinning around, Bracken vanished, leaving just a faint trail of sparkles in the air. Mia smiled. She knew he would come back as soon as she called his name. That was one of the many amazing things about Star Animals. They had the ability to disappear and reappear whenever they wanted. They tried to avoid being seen by people who weren't Star Friends, so being able to vanish was very useful.

Heaving on her backpack, Mia wriggled the straps over her shoulders and went downstairs.

Her mom and Violet's dad were talking by the front door. Her mom hugged her. "Bye, sweetheart. Have fun."

Mia squeezed her mom tightly, then hearing her friends calling her, she hurried to the car. Violet's dad followed and put her backpack in the front with the other bags while she climbed into the back next to Violet. Lexi and Sita were in the two extra seats in the way back of the car.

"It's vacation time at last!" said Sita excitedly as Violet's dad started the engine and drove off.

"I hope we get to go climbing," said Lexi.

"And swim in a stream," said Mia.

"And toast marshmallows around a campfire," said Sita.

Mia realized that Violet was being unusually quiet. "Are you okay, Violet?" she asked.

Violet was chewing her lower lip. "I don't know if I want to go after all," she admitted. "What if the food's horrible and there are bugs

in our tent?"

"It'll be fine," Lexi told her. "More than fine. It'll be fun!"

"I bet the food will be good," said Mia.

"And we'll get rid of any bugs for you," said Sita.

Mia reached out and squeezed Violet's hand. It was strange seeing her look so worried. In school, Violet was very confident, and in their magic adventures, she was usually the first to leap into action. But staying away from home for three nights without parents was quite a big deal, and none of them knew exactly what they'd be doing at camp. To Mia, that just made the vacation more exciting, but she knew Violet liked to know what to expect—and she really did hate bugs.

"Let's sing something!" Mia suggested to distract her. "How about 'Ninety-nine Bottles of Pop on the Wall'?" She launched enthusiastically into the song.

The countryside sped by. After "Ninety-nine Bottles of Pop on the Wall," they moved on to songs from when they were little, like "The Wheels on the Bus Go 'Round and 'Round," which they kept adding their own verses to.

Mia thought Violet's dad looked very relieved when they finally arrived at Maplewood Forest.

They drove past a farm with hundreds of chickens pecking around the fields and turned

into the forest. They went through the public
parking lot and bumped along a track between
fir trees, following the signs until they came
to an entrance to a smaller parking lot with a
wooden sign arching over it:

Maplewood Survival Skills Camp

"We're here!" Mia said, excitement
whooshing through her as she saw parents and
children milling around and talking to people
carrying clipboards, who were dressed in green
shorts and polo shirts with name badges. "Our
vacation's about to begin!"

3
SETTLING IN

Connie Joseph, the camp owner, was standing near the entrance. Her blond hair was in two short braids, and her face was tanned.

"Hi!" she said as Violet's dad put his window down. "If you could park over by those cones, that would be great, then check in with one of the camp guides."

The guides were dressed in khaki shorts and vests with a bunch of pockets. They were checking off names on their clipboards and helping children carry their luggage over to

a circle of logs around a campfire. Beyond the parking area there were a couple of sheds, a huge open-sided yurt with two long tables inside, an outdoor kitchen, and a wooden toilet block. Farther into the trees, there was an array of tents in a clearing, although they looked very different from the ones Mia had camped in before. Instead of being brightly colored and made of nylon, they were beige canvas bell tents with sides that could be rolled up.

Violet's dad began to unload all the bags while the girls scrambled out of the car and breathed in the pine-scented air. The forest looked very exciting, the tall trees clustering together as if they were hiding all kinds of secrets. Mia couldn't wait to call Bracken and see what he thought of it!

"There's Alyssa and Hannah," said Sita, pointing to two girls from their school chatting by the campfire.

"And Maddie Taylor," said Violet, nodding at a tall girl with long, dark brown hair held back by two barrettes who was sitting on her own. Maddie had joined Mia and Violet's class six weeks ago.

"There are a lot of people from school here," said Mia, noticing Brad and Tyler from Lexi and Sita's class.

Another car pulled up, and three boys from Mia and Violet's class jumped out.

"Hi everyone!" said Josh, patting his bag and grinning at them. "Hope you're ready to be pranked!"

"If you prank us, we'll get you back!" warned Lexi.

"Come and grab your things, girls," called Violet's dad.

They were just picking their bags up when an old jeep drove in through the gates. A gray-haired woman dressed in rain boots and a green jacket got out and began having a heated conversation with Connie. Connie seemed to be trying to calm her down.

After a few moments, the woman got back into her car and drove off again, looking angry.

"Everything okay?" asked Violet's dad curiously as Connie came over.

Connie let out a sigh. "I hope so. That was my neighbor—Mrs. Coates. She keeps free-range chickens on the farm that borders the forest. She's not very happy that I've started this camping business here, although I've told her the campers won't disturb her or her chickens. Hopefully, she'll come around soon when she finds that we're not going to be a nuisance. This is my first week."

After checking in, Mia and the others said good-bye to Violet's dad and joined the rest of the campers around the fire. Mia was surprised when she saw a familiar adult talking to Maddie—a young woman with black hair tied back in a thick ponytail who was wearing the same uniform as the other guides and had a name badge that read *Ginika Amadi*.

"It's Miss Amadi!" Mia hissed, nudging Violet.

"What's she doing here?" whispered Violet.

Miss Amadi was going to be Mia and Violet's new teacher when they went back after break because their regular teacher, Miss Harris, was leaving to have a baby. Miss Amadi had visited the class a few times before school

had let out, and Violet and Mia had decided she seemed nice.

"Hello, girls," Miss Amadi said, looking around and smiling. "Don't look so surprised. I'm still going to be your teacher at school! I'm just helping out here this week before I start full-time teaching," she explained. "Connie and I are friends, and she asked me if I could provide an extra pair of hands for her first week. I love being outdoors, so I jumped at the chance."

She patted the log beside her, inviting them to sit down.

"While we're at camp, you can call me Ginni, but when we're back at school you'll have to call me Miss Amadi."

Mia sat down shyly next to her. It felt a little strange having a teacher here, and she couldn't imagine calling her Ginni. It just felt wrong!

Connie brought the last of the campers over to the campfire.

Miss Amadi looked at her questioningly. "Did I see Mrs. Coates in the parking lot again?"

Connie nodded. "She's really not happy about us being here."

"I'll take her a peace offering of some chocolate brownies later," said Miss Amadi. "Hopefully she'll calm down soon."

"I really hope so," Connie said. "Anyway, time to get started." She banged a small drum, and all the campers fell silent. "Welcome to Maplewood, everyone. My name is Connie Joseph, and I'm in charge. If you have any problems, come and see me, or go to any of the guides. Their names are Jacob, Matt, Emma, and Ginni."

As she said their names, each adult stood up and waved.

"Now, time for some camp rules, and then we can have some fun!"

Connie told them that when she banged the drum, it meant they all had to gather around her, and she explained where the boundaries of the camp were.

"Definitely no going out of the forest into the fields. The farmer has free-range chickens and doesn't want them disturbed. The other boundaries are marked by red paint marks on trees."

She went on to remind them that no cell phones were allowed and pointed out the tents in the clearing behind the campfire.

"You'll be sleeping in groups of three or four. The five smaller tents in the center of the camping area are for the camp guides. I really hope you're going to have a wonderful time here, do plenty of fun things, and learn a lot about the forest. Now, your tents…." Connie checked her clipboard. "Tent One: Jack, Tyler, and Brad. Tent Two: Nikhil, Josh, and Dan.

Tent Three: Mia, Sita, Lexi, and Maddie."

Mia felt as if she'd just had a bucket of ice dumped over her. *Maddie and not Violet!* She glanced swiftly at her friends and saw they were all looking as shocked as she felt. Violet's hand had flown to her mouth.

"Tent Four: Violet, Alyssa, Hannah, and Anoushka," continued Connie.

Mia hardly listened. Her thoughts were racing. They had to do something! If Violet wasn't in the same tent as them, they wouldn't be able to have their Star Animals sleeping with them. But it wasn't just that. She also knew how worried Violet was about camping.

"Take your things to your tents," said Connie when she finished reading out the names. "Then there will be a fort-building session and a scavenger hunt before dinner."

Violet looked close to tears. "I don't want to be in a different tent. If I can't be with you, I'm going home!" she said.

"Don't panic. Let's talk to Connie," said Lexi quickly.

But Connie was already deep in discussion with some campers from another school who Mia didn't know. She spotted Miss Amadi heading toward one of the smaller single tents. "Let's ask Miss Amadi instead."

They hurried after the teacher, calling her name.

Miss Amadi stopped by her tent and looked around. "What is it, girls?"

They all tried to explain at once.

Miss Amadi held up her hands. "Whoa! Let me just get my water bottle and then one of you can tell me what's going on."

She ducked into her tent. The entrance flap was rolled up, and Mia could see that the tent was very cozy inside. Miss Amadi had an inflatable bed, and there was a patterned throw with giraffes laid over her sleeping bag. There was a rag rug on the floor and three wooden crates that were being used as tables with bright scarves draped over them.

"I like your tent," said Sita.

"Thanks." Miss Amadi smiled as she picked up her water bottle from one of the crates. "I've been traveling around the world this year, collecting little souvenirs wherever I go."

She waved at a crate near her bed that had a stand in the shape of a tree with bracelets and necklaces hanging from it, some animal ornaments, and a cuddly sloth.

"I always like to make the place I'm staying

in feel like home." She came back out and took a drink of water. "Now, tell me what the problem is."

Mia explained about Violet not being in the same tent as them.

Miss Amadi looked guilty. "Oh, dear, this is my fault. I noticed Maddie sitting on her own and thought she looked lonely, so I went to check that she was okay. She told me she doesn't really have any friends at school, but she did mention that you'd been friendly, Mia, and that she'd put you down on her application form as someone she'd like to share a tent with. So I asked Connie to swap Maddie and Violet. I didn't think you'd mind, Violet."

"Oh." Mia didn't know quite what to say. She didn't want to upset Maddie, but she was really worried that Violet would insist on going home if she couldn't share with them.

"Can they swap?" asked Lexi. "Alyssa, Hannah, and Anoushka are really nice. I'm sure

Maddie will have fun with them."

"It's not that we don't like Maddie," Mia said quickly. "It's just we really wanted to be together and—" she shot a look at Violet— "Violet's a little nervous about camping."

"If I can't be with the others, I don't want to stay," said Violet unhappily.

"Oh, Violet," said Miss Amadi. "If I'd known sharing a tent with Mia, Sita, and Lexi was so important to you, I'd never have suggested the swap. Don't worry—I'll sort this out. You and Maddie can change places. But why are you feeling so nervous?"

"I've never been camping before," Violet admitted. "I'm worried about sleeping in a tent and doing stuff like fishing, and I definitely don't want to have to climb trees. I hate heights."

"If you're really worried about an activity, you won't have to do it," Miss Amadi reassured her. "And we're not just going to do things like climb trees and fish. You'll also learn about

the forest, the animals who live here, the tracks they leave, the plants you find. You'll like that, won't you?"

Violet nodded. She did love learning about things.

"You'll have a wonderful time—I know it. Look."

Miss Amadi glanced around and then went back into the tent and picked up a carved wooden monkey from the crate near her bed. It had a big smile on its friendly face and fluffy ears sticking out of the side of its head.

"My aunt in Nigeria gave this to me when I visited her in the summer. She told me he's very good at taking care of people. What do we think, Aaya?" she said, pretending to talk to the monkey. "Will you take care of Violet and help her have a good time while she's here at camp?"

She waggled the monkey from side to side and spoke in a silly voice as if it were answering her. "*Oh, yes. Oh, yes. I promise I will!*"

Mia exchanged
looks with the
others. It was
really nice of
Miss Amadi to
try and cheer
Violet up, but
they weren't
babies!

Miss Amadi
bopped Violet gently
on the nose with the monkey and plonked him
in her hands. "Here, Violet, you can keep Aaya
while you're at camp and see if he helps."

Violet managed a faint smile and handed
the monkey back. "Thanks, Miss Amadi, but as
long as I'm in the same tent as Mia, Lexi, and
Sita, I'll be fine."

"Okay, well, let's get that sorted then," said
Miss Amadi with a smile. She put the monkey
back and led the way over to the girls' tent,

where Maddie was just carrying her bag inside.

Maddie looked a little upset when she heard about the swap, but Alyssa, Hannah, and Anoushka came to help her move her things, and Mia watched them all walking back across the clearing to Tent Four, chatting and laughing.

"Phew!" she said, letting the flap of their tent close. "Maddie looks happy."

Violet, Sita, and Lexi were laying their sleeping bags out on the thick foam mats that would be their beds for the next three nights. They each had an empty wooden crate with a lid to store their things in and an extra blanket on top. There was a rug on the floor and a plastic sheet outside for keeping their muddy boots on.

"And now it's just the four of us like we planned."

Lexi grinned. "Don't you mean the eight of us?" She called Juniper's name.

There was a swirl of starry light, and the

little red squirrel appeared. He scampered up the center pole in the tent. Mia, Violet, and Sita quickly called their animals, too.

Bracken bounced around Mia, while Sorrel wove around Violet's legs, purring, and Willow cuddled against Sita's side. Bracken jumped into Mia's arms, his soft, russet-red fur tickling her chin and his cold black nose pressing against her cheek.

"I like this tent!" said Juniper, taking a flying leap on to Lexi's head and playing with her dark curls. "It's has a climbing pole!"

Sorrel looked around. "Where are the beds?"

"There," said Violet, pointing to the foam pad where her sleeping bag was.

"You want me to sleep on *that?*" Sorrel said in horror.

"Poor princess pussycat," teased Bracken. "Don't you want to sleep on the ground?"

Sorrel stalked over to the crate beside Violet's bed. "You can sleep on the ground, Fox, but I—" she jumped up on to the fleecy blanket on top of Violet's crate—"shall sleep here."

She sat down as if she were on a throne, her nose in the air and her long tail dangling.

Bracken couldn't resist. He darted forward and tweaked the end of her tail with his teeth. Sorrel gave an outraged yowl and leaped up, the fur rising along her back.

"Bracken, don't tease Sorrel!" said Mia,

shaking her head and trying not to smile. Bracken loved to wind Sorrel up.

Violet soothed the wildcat. "It's okay, Sorrel. Calm down."

Sorrel's coat slowly flattened. Giving a grumpy huff, she curled up like a doughnut on the blanket, glaring at Bracken and wrapping her tail safely around her paws.

They unpacked their things. As Mia took a small, round folding mirror out of her backpack, she paused.

Bracken seemed to read her mind. "Are you thinking of doing some magic, Mia?" he asked eagerly.

Each of the girls could do different things
when they connected to the magic current.
Lexi could become super agile and sense
when the others were in danger. Sita could
heal wounds and make people and spirits do
whatever she wanted—although she didn't like
that power and only used it in times of real
danger. Violet could shadow-travel and disguise
things, including herself, as well as command
spirits to return to the realms they had come
from. Mia could use shiny surfaces to see
things happening elsewhere, get glimpses of the
past and the future, and create invisible magic
shields. Doing magic felt amazing!

"I could take a quick look with my seeing
magic," Mia said with a grin. "I mean, just to
check that there isn't anything magical going
on here that we should know about, like
someone doing dark magic and summoning
Shades."

Shades were evil spirits conjured from the

shadows. They could be trapped in everyday objects and loved to manipulate people and cause trouble and unhappiness. There were all kinds of Shades—Mirror Shades, who could make people become jealous; Fear Shades, who could terrify people by making them think their deepest fears were coming true; Wish Shades and Heart's Desire Shades, who granted wishes but who did it in a way that caused pain and unhappiness to others. There were so many different types, and they were all horrible.

Since Mia and the others had become Star Friends, they had sent plenty of Shades back to the shadows as well as stopping people who had been causing trouble, using the magic in plants and crystals.

Mia didn't think for a moment that there would be any bad magic to worry about at camp but she loved doing magic, so she sat down on her mattress with her mirror anyway. With Bracken cuddling up against her, she

gazed into the shining surface and silently asked the magic, *Please show me if there is anything magical going on here.*

Her body tingled as the current started to run through her. The trickle of magic became a flood until she felt as if every cell in her body were filled with a wonderful sparkling power. The surface of the mirror began to swirl, and images appeared in it! She saw a cute brown otter, the tents in the camp clearing, a woman knocking on a front door in a porch filled with house plants in pots.... The images flicked past quickly! An animal with a long tail jumping through the treetops, broken branches littering a sunny glade of slender firs, a smoldering campfire, two black eyes peering out of lush foliage....

The images faded, and Mia lowered the mirror.

"Did you see anything?" asked Bracken eagerly.

"I did," Mia said, unease prickling through her.

The others turned to look at her. "You did?" Violet said.

Sorrel sat up, suddenly awake. "Well, spit it out, girl. What did you see?"

With the others listening intently, Mia described the images. "I don't know if the things the magic showed me have happened already or might happen in the future."

"Whichever they are, it sounds like there's definitely some magic going on here," Lexi said excitedly.

"The air does smell like it," said Willow, snuffing deeply. She and Sorrel had the ability to smell when Shades were nearby, and they were very sensitive to the scent of other magic, too.

"You can smell a Shade?" Sita said in alarm.

Sorrel shook her head. "Not a Shade." She sniffed delicately. "There are a few different kinds of magic, some that seem familiar, but also a magic I do not recognize."

Sita sighed. "Oh, I hope there isn't any bad magic going on here. I just want to have a fun vacation."

"It'll be even more fun if there's dark magic we have to stop," said Violet, her green eyes sparkling. "It'll make things much more exciting."

Mia grinned at her. "So you're not still thinking about going home?"

Violet grinned back. "No way! Not when there's a mystery to solve!"

4
SHELTERS AND A SCAVENGER HUNT

A drum banged outside the tent. "That's Connie calling us. We'd better go," Mia said to the animals.

"While you're gone, we'll explore and see if we can find out more about the magic," said Bracken.

"Okay, but be careful," said Mia. "Try not to be seen." Although all four animals were the kind of animals that might be found in a forest, Mia was sure the adults would think it was strange if they started showing up all the time!

"We will." Bracken put his paws on her knees and licked her nose. "Call us as soon as you can. I'll miss you!"

The girls put on their boots and went to join the rest of the campers.

"It's time for you to learn how to build shelters!" Connie told them. "Emma, Matt, and Jacob are going to be in charge, so make sure you do what they say."

The campers set off with the three guides while Connie stayed in camp to prepare dinner and Miss Amadi took some brownies over to the grumpy farmer to try to smooth things over.

Emma, Jacob, and Matt stopped in a glade surrounded by tall fir trees at the edge of camp. The sun shone down through the branches, casting tiger stripes of light on the forest floor. Mia frowned. It felt weirdly familiar. She shook her head. It must be her imagination playing tricks on her.

The guides demonstrated how to construct

a frame for a shelter by tying thick fallen
branches together using a variety of knots.

"It's time for you to build your own
shelters," said Emma. "You can start now and
finish tomorrow. If your shelters are sturdy
enough, then anyone who wants to can sleep
in their shelter on the final night."

"Do we have to?" said Violet.

"It'll be fun!" said Emma, but Violet didn't
look convinced.

They all set about gathering what they
needed. As Mia was pulling a large fir tree branch
out of the undergrowth, she caught sight of
Bracken's fluffy face peeking mischievously
at her from between some brambles.
She grinned but waved at him
to go away before anyone saw
him. Turning, he disappeared
into the undergrowth with
a flick of his white-tipped
bushy tail.

"Emma! I just saw a red squirrel!" exclaimed one of the campers. "It ran up that tree."

"It wouldn't have been a red squirrel, Sophie," said Emma. "There aren't any in this area."

Sophie looked puzzled. "But it looked really red."

"Gray squirrels often have a chestnut tinge to their coats, so that's probably what you saw," said Emma.

"I spotted a little deer," said Alyssa. "It was hiding behind those trees."

The girls exchanged alarmed looks. Their animals were really going to have to work harder at not being seen!

"There are all kinds of animals living in this forest," said Jacob.

"I just saw a monkey," said Dan.

Jacob laughed. "You wouldn't have seen a monkey, Dan. There aren't any wild monkeys out here, but there are many other animals, so keep your eyes peeled."

"And look for their tracks," said Emma. "I found some otter prints by the stream this morning. There's a poster in the yurt with different animal tracks if you want to identify any you find."

Jacob clapped his hands. "Get going on those shelters!"

When the structure was finished, the campers started to fill in the sides with leafy branches.

Violet poked the shelter that she and the others were making. It wobbled alarmingly. "I'm really not sure I want to sleep in that," she said doubtfully. "It looks like it might fall down at any moment."

"You can add some more struts tomorrow and tie everything together more firmly," said Emma, overhearing. "But now it's time for the scavenger hunt!"

She and the other guides handed out a list of things the children had to find, bags to put the items in, and walkie-talkies to each team.

"The team who finds the most items is the winner. If more than one team find all the items, it's the first team back to camp who wins," Emma said.

"Make sure you stay within the camp boundaries," said Matt. "No going past the red marks on the trees. If you need us, call on the walkie-talkies."

"We'll see you back at the campfire at—"

Jacob checked his watch—"six o'clock at the latest. Go ahead!"

Everyone clustered into their groups.

Mia read out the list. "Okay, so we need to find: one gray stone, one white stone, four different leaves, a pine cone, an acorn, a white petal, brown fern, and three different feathers."

"We could call the animals and get them to help," Violet whispered. "Then we'd be back first and win!"

"Good idea," said Lexi.

"But that would be cheating," protested Sita.

"Sita's right. No magic, okay?" said Mia.

Lexi and Violet sighed. They were both very competitive.

They set off and spotted the stones they needed in the nearby stream. Then they found three feathers lying on the track. Farther down the path, there was a clump of old brown fern.

"How lucky is that?" said Violet, scooping it

up. "Here. Put everything in the bag, Lexi."

"We still need leaves, a white flower petal, a pine cone, and an acorn," Sita said.

There was a rustle in the undergrowth. Mia looked around.

"I bet there are some acorns under the oak trees over there. Come on!" said Lexi. She ran off with Violet and Sita.

Mia was about to follow when she heard another rustle. Wondering whether it was one of their animals watching them, she went closer and spotted a white flower caught in the brambles. Taking a petal, she paused. It was strange that they kept finding everything they needed.

She peered into the bushes. "Bracken?" she called softly. "Is that you?" There was a rustle farther back in the undergrowth, and she saw the branches move.

"Please don't help us. I don't want to win by cheating," she whispered.

There was no more movement or sound. Mia dropped the petal she'd found on the ground. They could find another white flower without Bracken's help.

She caught up with the others, and after a bit of searching, found the pine cone, acorn, and leaves. When they came across a vine with big white flowers, they took a single petal and raced back to camp only to find that Dan, Nikhil, and Josh had just beaten them to it.

"You're too late!" Josh said triumphantly.

"What took you so long?" teased Nikhil.

Violet and Lexi looked a little grumpy.

"How long have you been back?" Mia asked the boys.

"Only about five minutes," admitted Dan. "By the way, you might want to be careful." He glanced at Nikhil and Josh. "When we were going into our tent, we saw a huge beetle crawl into yours."

"A beetle?" echoed Violet nervously.

"A really big one!" said Nikhil, nodding.

"Yeah, sure," said Mia disbelievingly.

"I don't want to sleep in our tent if there's a beetle in there," Violet said.

"I bet there isn't really one," said Mia.

"There is, and it's huge," said Nikhil.

Violet squeaked in alarm.

"Well, I'm not scared of beetles," said Lexi.

"Me neither," said Sita. "Let's go and check, Violet."

They walked over to their tent with the boys following.

"There's absolutely nothing here," said Mia as she, Lexi, and Sita raised the foam mattresses and checked under the sleeping bags. "I told you the boys are just…." Lifting her pillow, she caught sight of a huge black beetle as big as her hand. She shrieked and leaped back, hearing an explosion of laughter at the entrance to the tent.

Almost immediately, she realized it was a prank. Her heart slowed down and she grabbed the rubber beetle. "Ha ha! Very funny!" she said, waving it at the boys.

They were clutching their sides. "You're right, it was!" chortled Josh.

"You should have seen your face, Mia!" gasped Nikhil.

Mia saw the funny side and she, Lexi, and Sita all joined in with the laughter.

"We'll get you back, you know," Mia said, throwing the beetle at Josh's head.

Chuckling, he caught it, and the three boys walked off.

"We really have to prank them back!" Lexi said.

"How?" asked Sita.

"I'm not sure yet, but I'll think of something!" Lexi promised.

5
STRANGE
HAPPENINGS

At dinnertime, everyone sat around the campfire and ate hot dogs and baked beans followed by chocolate brownies.

"See, I told you there was no need to worry about the food," Mia said to Violet as they washed their plates in a big trough of soapy water and left them on a wooden drying rack. "It's really nice."

"Tonight's was," said Violet. "But I asked Connie what we're having tomorrow and she said salmon, rice, and broccoli. I don't like

salmon—or broccoli!"

"Then just eat the rice and pudding," said Mia.

Violet made a face. "She also said we're all going to cook our own dinner on the campfire. But what if someone starts messing around near it or stands too close to the flames or the cooking attracts bugs…?"

"Violet, relax!" said Mia as they went back to the fire. "It'll be fine."

Just then, there was the sound of a car pulling into the parking area. The adults looked at each other in surprise.

"I wonder who that is," Connie said, getting to her feet.

A car door slammed, and a woman came stomping toward them. Mia saw that it was the chicken farmer. She had a bulging bag over one shoulder.

"Mrs. Coates," said Connie, going to meet her. "Can I help you?"

"You certainly can!" snapped the farmer. "You can help by keeping these children—" she swung her arm around, gesturing at the campers— "away from my chickens!"

"But no one's been near your chickens—" Connie began.

"They most certainly have!" snapped Mrs. Coates. "I saw two boys climbing into one of my fields just a few hours ago!"

"Oh my goodness," said Connie in dismay. "I really am very sorry. It must have been during the scavenger hunt." She looked at the campers. "Did someone go out of the forest and into the fields?"

One of the boys Mia didn't know sheepishly put his hand up. "I'm sorry. I think that was me and Ashton. We saw a feather in the grass and thought it wouldn't matter if we took it. There weren't any chickens in the field."

"All fields are out of bounds," Connie said. "Do you understand?"

Everyone nodded.

"I'm sorry. It won't happen again," Connie told Mrs. Coates.

"It had better not," the farmer said crossly. "And you can take these things back!" She pulled a plastic box and a pottery animal out of her bag and pushed them into Connie's hands. "Leaving things by my front door! It's just not right!"

Connie looked confused. "Ginni dropped off the brownies this afternoon. We thought you might like them, but…." She held up the yard ornament—it was a raccoon sitting up on its back legs, holding an acorn made out of a glittering pink crystal. "I've never seen this before in my life."

Mrs. Coates snorted and stomped away. Slamming the car door, she drove off.

"Well," Connie said, looking very taken aback, "I have no idea why she thought this had come from us."

She raised the raccoon. It had pricked, pointed ears and shining black eyes that looked beseechingly out from the dark mask-like markings on its face. A long tail curved up behind it, and its little human-like hands were holding the pink crystal shaped like an acorn, which had some words engraved on it.

Connie read them out loud. "*I bring the gift of friendship.*"

Miss Amadi smiled. "Let's not turn that down." She took the raccoon from Connie and placed it on one of the log seats. "If Mrs. Coates doesn't want him, he can have a home here."

While the guides handed out sticks, marshmallows, chocolate, and graham crackers so the campers could make s'mores, Mia went over to examine the pottery animal. Earlier on, Willow and Sorrel had said they could smell different kinds of magic, and crystals had magic in them that could be used for good or bad. Could the raccoon's crystal acorn be magical?

Miss Amadi joined her. "He's cute, isn't he?

I wonder how he showed up on Mrs. Coates's porch." She picked up the raccoon. "Well, if the grumpy old lady doesn't want you, I'll keep you!" she said to it. She handed a stick to Mia. "Here you go—it's s'mores time!"

After everyone had made s'mores by squishing toasted marshmallows and chocolate between graham crackers, Jacob and Miss Amadi got their guitars out, and everyone sang songs. Even Violet seemed to enjoy the evening. As the sun set, the solar-powered lanterns in the trees lit up, and Connie handed out fleece blankets to keep them warm.

Despite the chill in the smoky air, Mia felt a glow of happiness as she and the others finally made their way to their tent at bedtime. Each tent also had a lantern outside to light the way.

They sat down on the plastic sheet outside and took their walking boots off. Connie had told them to leave them by the entrance flap so that they could find them easily if they wanted to use the bathroom during the night. The girls lined their boots up neatly and went inside, turning their flashlights on so they could see.

"Bed at last!" said Lexi, flopping onto her sleeping bag.

"Let's get into our pajamas and call the animals," said Sita. "I really want to see Willow."

They got changed and called the animals' names—Bracken, Willow, Juniper, and Sorrel— each of them appearing in a shimmer of stars. After enthusiastically greeting the girls, they snuggled down on the beds or, in Sorrel's case, on top of the crate beside Violet's bed.

"You're really going to have to try harder not to be seen by other people!" said Mia, tickling Bracken's soft, downy tummy as he rolled over on his back on her sleeping bag.

"Yes, Sophie looked very confused when Emma told her there were no red squirrels here!" said Lexi with a grin as Juniper sat on her shoulder, chattering softly.

"And thanks for trying to help with the
scavenger hunt today," Mia said to Bracken.
"But it's cheating if we use magic in a
competition."

Bracken wriggled up, looking surprised. "I
didn't help you."

"None of us did," said Willow.

Mia frowned. "So you didn't put the feathers
or fern on the track? Or leave the flower in the
brambles for me to find?"

"If you came across things, it certainly wasn't because of us," said Sorrel sharply. "While you were on your hunt, we were busy exploring the camp."

"Did you find anything?" Lexi asked eagerly.

"We did smell magic near the tents," said Willow.

"I think it's stronger now," said Sorrel, sniffing. "Closer."

"Could it be crystal magic you're smelling?" Mia asked, thinking about the raccoon.

"Yes," said Willow thoughtfully. "I did smell crystal magic but also other magic, too. Not Shades, though," she said, nuzzling Sita, who looked relieved. "And it might not be bad magic. It could just be someone with crystals or other objects that they don't know are magical."

"Still, someone *could* be planning on doing something bad with magic," said Violet. "We must keep a lookout."

"Definitely!" said Mia.

"What's happening tomorrow?" Bracken asked. "Can we all go exploring together?"

"I don't think so," Mia said, remembering what Connie had said before they went to bed. "There are lots of activities with the other campers. Tree-climbing and more shelter-building in the morning, then in the afternoon we're fishing in the stream and learning how to cook on the campfire."

Violet shuddered. "I don't want to do any of those things. This evening's actually been fun, but I'm not looking forward to tomorrow." She looked around. "Or to sleeping in this tent. What if beetles or spiders or mice come in?"

"Don't worry, Violet," Sorrel reassured her. "If I see a mouse in here, I'll eat it!"

"No!" Mia, Lexi, and Sita exclaimed.

"If you see a mouse, you can't kill it, Sorrel," said Sita. "Just guide it out of the tent."

Sorrel looked surprised. "But Violet might like a nice mouse head for breakfast."

"I really wouldn't," said Violet hastily.

"Ooh," said Lexi suddenly. "Mice! That's just given me an idea for a prank we could play on the boys."

"What kind of prank?" said Mia eagerly.

"I'll tell you tomorrow. I need to see what's in the kitchen first," said Lexi.

Sita yawned. "I'm tired. Let's go to sleep."

"What about our midnight snack?" said Mia.

"Tomorrow," said Violet, yawning like Sita.

Mia felt a little disappointed, but as she snuggled down farther into her warm sleeping bag, she had to admit she was feeling pretty tired, too. "Okay, night, everyone," she said as they all turned their flashlights off.

"Night," the others murmured.

Bracken snuggled into Mia's arms, and burying her face in his soft fur, she fell asleep.

Mia dreamed she was in the forest on her own. Her spine tingled and she swung around, sure something was watching her. She saw a shadow leaping through the tree branches high above. Her heart pounded.

"Juniper?" she called. But the little red squirrel didn't come scampering down the tree.

Mia looked up and saw two small hands holding the branches apart while two bright black eyes peered at her through the gap in the leaves.

Feeling a wave of alarm, she started to hurry down the forest path. Above her, the creature followed, high up in the trees....

Mia sat up in bed, her heart racing. It was very dark in the tent. She could hear Lexi, Sita, and Violet breathing softly in their sleep. She shook her head to clear the bad dream away, trying to ignore the anxiety that was worming its way inside her. Her dreams often warned her when there was danger coming.

It might not have been a magical dream, she told herself. *It could have just been a normal one.* She began to snuggle back down in her warm sleeping bag but stopped when she heard a rustle outside the tent. She froze. It sounded like someone was creeping around out there.

Mia's heart started to race again.

Bracken, who had moved down the bed to sleep by her feet, stirred and sat up. "Is everything all right, Mia?"

"I think there's someone outside the tent," she hissed.

"I'll go and check," said Bracken, vanishing. A minute later, he reappeared. "There's no one there. You must have imagined it."

Mia breathed out in relief. "Phew." She lay down, and he cuddled up next to her. She put her arms around him. "I'm so glad you're here with me," she whispered.

Bracken snuggled closer. "I wouldn't want to be anywhere else."

6
MORE THAN
JUST PRANKS

Mia was woken in the morning by Lexi
shaking her shoulder. "Time for breakfast and
tree-climbing!"

Mia sat up, rubbing the sleep from her eyes.
The sun was coming up, lighting the inside of
the tent, and she could feel the fears from the
night fading. She pulled on her clothes.

"Where are our boots?" said Sita as they
stepped out onto the plastic sheet

They all looked around in surprise. Their
boots were gone!

"It's probably the boys playing another prank," said Lexi.

Mia groaned. "I heard a noise outside during the night. Bracken checked, but by the time he got outside, there was no one there."

"What should we do?" said Violet. "We can't go to breakfast in our slippers." The grass was thick with early-morning dew.

Mia noticed Maddie sitting on the plastic sheet in front of her tent nearby. "Maddie, you haven't seen our boots, have you?" she called.

Maddie shook her head shyly. "I'm sorry. No."

"It has to be the boys," said Lexi. "Hey, Dan! Nikhil! Josh!" she shouted at the tent next door. "Give us our boots back!"

There was a pause and then Dan looked out, his hair messed up. "What are you yelling about?"

"Our boots!" said Violet.

"Can we have them back now, please?" said Sita.

Dan looked confused. "Um…."

"Don't act like you don't know where they are," said Mia, putting her hands on her hips. "We can't get breakfast until we have them."

"But we didn't take them," said Dan. He saw the disbelief on their faces. "Honestly. We didn't."

Mia frowned. He actually looked like he was telling the truth.

"Well, someone did," said Lexi, peering around. "Whoever took our boots, give them back *right now!*" she shouted.

Miss Amadi appeared from the trees behind the tent. "What's going on, girls?" she asked.

They told her about their missing boots. Miss Amadi sighed. "Oh, dear. It sounds like a prank."

She went around to all the tents. Campers emerged sleepily, in the middle of getting dressed. They all shook their heads when Miss Amadi asked them about the girls' boots.

She came back, looking mystified. "No one has them."

Just then Matt and Jacob came through the trees.

They were holding four pairs of dripping-wet boots.

"Our boots!" exclaimed Lexi.

"Someone put them in the stream," said Jacob.

"We found them when we were getting water."

"This isn't right," Miss Amadi said, looking around at the campers. "Pranks are all well and good, but now Lexi, Mia, Violet, and Sita aren't going to be able to do anything until their boots dry out. Who did this?"

Mia tried to spot someone looking guilty, but no one owned up.

"Pranks like this must stop. Do you understand?" Miss Amadi said.

Everyone nodded.

Miss Amadi turned to Mia and the others. "I'll stuff your boots with newspaper and put them by the embers of the fire to dry them out. If I give you some plastic bags, you can put them over your slippers and come to breakfast. I'm afraid you won't be able to join in with the tree-climbing, though. You can't do that in your slippers."

Violet looked very relieved.

Miss Amadi took their boots away, and the

girls sat down on the plastic sheet.

"What a rotten prank. Now we can't go climbing," said Lexi crossly.

"It would have been fine if whoever did it had just hidden our boots," said Sita. "Why did they have to put them in the stream?"

"Do you think it was the boys?" said Mia.

Lexi shook her head. "They're really annoying at times, but they're not mean."

"What about Maddie?" Violet said. "She was up before we were. Maybe she wanted to get back at us because she had to change tents."

"No," Mia said quickly. "I'm sure she wouldn't do something like that. Whenever I've spoken to her, she's seemed nice."

They waited until Miss Amadi came back with plastic bags and tape. She helped them secure the bags over their slippers. As Mia stood up, she noticed a couple of marks on the ground. There was one that looked like a small handprint and a couple that looked like little footprints.

"Are they animal tracks?" she asked Miss Amadi.

Miss Amadi examined them. "Possibly, but I'm not very good at identifying animals from their tracks. They could be from a squirrel or maybe a rat."

"A rat?" Violet said in alarm.

"It was probably a squirrel," said Mia quickly, not wanting Violet to be freaked out by the thought of a rat near their tent.

"Oh, *a squirrel*," said Violet in relief, and Mia knew she was thinking about Juniper.

She grinned at her. "Who knows? We may find some fox, deer, and cat prints, too!"

They headed over to the yurt for breakfast. Mia had been hoping they'd have sausages again, but the fire had been put out overnight for safety reasons, and so it was just fruit and oatmeal.

After breakfast, it was time for tree-climbing near the tents. The guides started off by

showing everyone how to climb safely, and then the campers had a turn. Mia and the others sat with Miss Amadi.

"It's boring just watching," sighed Lexi.

"We don't have to just sit here doing nothing," said Miss Amadi. "I was thinking about Mrs. Coates last night and how much better it would be if there could be a friendly relationship between her and Connie. How about we make some toys for her chickens?"

"Toys? For chickens?" Mia echoed.

Miss Amadi nodded enthusiastically. "Chickens love to perch and have things to peck at. We could make chicken gyms from tree branches and fruit-and-vegetable garlands for them to peck at—you can use apples that are bruised, the outer leaves of cabbages and lettuces, things like that. I'm sure we can find that kind of stuff in the store cupboard. What do you think?"

The girls all nodded. It sounded better than just watching the others climb. They found

several sturdy branches while Miss Amadi
gathered some rope and strong scissors. Then
she showed them how to tie the branches
together. By break time, they
had constructed two jungle
gyms and three long fruit-
and-vegetable garlands.

"It's a good way to use
up fruit and veggies
that would
otherwise be
thrown away
or composted,"
said Miss Amadi.
"Maybe if Connie
and Mrs. Coates become
friends, this could be a regular thing."

After the break, they had a lesson on
identifying trees, and then it was time for more
work on their shelters. The girls' boots were
still damp inside, so Connie suggested that they

put plastic bags over their socks to keep their feet dry inside their boots so they could join in.

With their feet crackling slightly in the plastic bags, they headed to the glade with the other campers. It was a beautiful warm day, and rays of sunlight were slanting through the tree canopy.

Mia felt very happy. She linked arms with Lexi. "This is great, isn't it?"

Lexi grinned at her. "Yep, I love camping."

"Me, too," said Sita. "It's wonderful being outside all the time."

"I've been thinking about the prank to play on the boys," said Lexi. "I saw some wild rice in the store cupboard when we were making the chicken garlands. It's black and looks just like mouse droppings. How about we put some on the boys' beds and pillows?"

Mia grinned. "Oh, yes!"

Just then, they heard shouting from up ahead. "The shelters!"

Mia and the others broke into a run.

Reaching the glade, they stopped in shock. The leafy branches had been pulled from the outside of the shelters, leaving just the structures beneath; the fern had been hauled out from inside; and the glade was now littered with debris.

"Oh, no!" cried Sita, running over to where their shelter had been. Other people's shelters were damaged, but theirs was lying in pieces on the ground, completely destroyed!

7
CAMPFIRE CHAOS

"Our shelter is ruined!" said Lexi in dismay, staring at the broken branches.

A memory tweaked at the corner of Mia's mind as she looked around the glade. There was something about the scene that seemed very familiar. What was it?

"Who did this?" Jacob demanded. No one put their hand up.

"Maybe it wasn't any of these guys, Jake," said Matt quickly. "They've been with us all morning."

"I was up doing yoga first thing," said Emma. "I didn't see anyone leave their tent before breakfast."

"I guess it could have been people walking through the forest and messing around," said Jacob. He sighed. "Looks like everyone needs to start rebuilding."

"I don't think we'll be sleeping in our shelter tomorrow night," said Lexi as she surveyed the mess of broken branches.

"What a shame," said Violet, not sounding like she meant it at all.

Sita glanced in Mia's direction. "Are you okay, Mia?"

"Hmm?" Mia said distractedly. She had been looking around, trying to figure out why the scene seemed so familiar. Suddenly, she remembered. "I saw the glade like this when I used the magic current last night!" She pulled the others into a huddle. "This was one of the things it showed me. Do you think that means

magic could be to blame?"

"It *is* the kind of horrible thing a Shade would do," Sita said, her brown eyes widening.

"But Willow and Sorrel said they couldn't smell any Shades," Violet pointed out.

"Maybe one came during the night," said Lexi.

Sita shuddered. "I hope not."

"Come on, guys," said Jacob, clapping his hands and coming over to them. "Less chatting, more working!"

Exchanging looks that said *we'll talk about this later*, they kept on with the shelter.

As Mia sorted the branches into piles of those that could be used again and those that were too broken, she noticed some tracks on a patch of bare ground. They were just like the ones she had seen by their tent that morning—marks that looked like they'd been made by something with little human-like hands and feet.

"Emma!" she called. "What are these?"

Emma examined them. "They're…."

She frowned and inspected them from several different angles. "You know, I'm not sure. Why don't you take a look at the poster in the yurt at lunchtime and see if you can find out?"

Mia nodded, and picking up a branch, took another look at the tracks. Was it a coincidence that the same strange tracks had appeared both here and by their tent? Excitement prickled down her spine—or was it a clue?

Mia wanted to talk to the others alone, but when they got back to camp, they were

ushered straight into the yurt for a lunch of
sandwiches, chips, and fruit. Spotting the poster
that had pictures of different animal tracks, Mia
went over to examine it.

There were no tracks that matched the ones
she'd seen. The handprints were a little like the
tracks rats and squirrels made with their front
paws, but the footprints were different. In the
tracks Mia had seen, the foot had a big toe that
looked almost like a thumb. She frowned. What
could have made them?

Miss Amadi came over, pulling her out of her
thoughts. "I took the chicken toys and garlands
to Mrs. Coates before lunch."

"Did she like them?" Mia asked.

Miss Amadi made a face. "Hard to tell. I think
she was surprised. She said a quick thank you and
then shut the door, but maybe the friendly gesture
will help." She sighed. "I really hope it does."

Mia was eager to talk to the others about the
tracks and about having seen the glade with the

shelters destroyed in her dream, but as soon as lunch was finished, Miss Amadi organized a game of kickball. Then they all had to go to the stream with Emma, Matt, and Jacob to learn how to fish.

I'll talk to them before dinner, Mia thought.

To their relief, the only fish they caught were little sticklebacks that they were told to immediately release again. At five o'clock, everyone headed back to camp to cook salmon, bought in the supermarket, over the fire.

"Connie should have the fire going by now—it needs to be good and hot to cook on," Emma said as they walked through the trees.

"Is that smoke?" Matt said, pointing in the direction of the camp. Looking up, they saw a big cloud billowing above the tree canopy. The guides exchanged alarmed looks.

"I'll stay here with the campers. You go ahead and see what's going on," Emma said to Matt and Jacob. They nodded and sprinted off.

"Okay, keep calm, everyone!" Emma called. "I'm sure everything's fine, but we'll just wait here for now."

"What if it's a fire?" Violet said in alarm.

"Then we'll follow the fire procedure, evacuate from camp, and call the fire department," Emma said. "Don't worry."

A few minutes later, they heard Matt shouting to them. "It's okay! You can all come back—it's safe!"

They hurried through the trees and saw that the campfire was now a smoking heap of damp logs. Mia stopped in her tracks. She'd seen the smoldering campfire with her magic just like she'd seen the destroyed shelters!

Two large barrels were lying on their sides next to the fire. Connie and Miss Amadi were standing with Jacob and Matt. They were all shaking their heads and looked shocked.

"What happened?" Emma exclaimed.

"The water barrels that collect rainwater

tipped onto the fire, putting it out," said Matt.

"I was in the kitchen area when I heard a huge bang," said Connie. "I came out and saw this!" She waved at the fire.

Miss Amadi frowned. "But how can the barrels have just fallen over?"

"They couldn't have," said Jacob grimly. "Someone must have pushed them. Maybe the same person who wrecked the shelters."

Connie rubbed her forehead, looking very upset. "Why would anyone do such horrible things?"

Miss Amadi hugged her. "I have no idea."

"It's almost like someone is trying to sabotage the camp," said Matt.

The adults exchanged worried looks.

"What should we do?" said Connie.

"I suppose all we can do is get the fire started again and keep a lookout for anything else happening," said Miss Amadi.

Emma nodded and turned to the campers. "Okay, everyone, we need to collect a bunch of wood to get the fire going."

"It won't be hot enough to cook on tonight," said Connie, "so it'll be pizza for dinner."

There was a chorus of delighted cheers. It seemed that Violet wasn't the only one who hadn't been looking forward to salmon for dinner!

As everyone began collecting sticks, Mia pulled at the others' arms. She couldn't wait to talk to them any longer. "We need to talk!" she hissed. "Right now!"

8
WHO COULD IT BE?

Mia was almost bursting with the news by the time they got back to their tent. They called the animals, and the words tumbled out of her. "I saw the glade with the wrecked shelters and the smoldering campfire yesterday with my magic! I think the adults are right and someone's trying to cause trouble here at camp, and I think they're doing it by using dark magic."

Sorrel hissed, Willow pawed the ground, and Juniper chattered uneasily.

"What kind of dark magic?" Sita said.

Bracken put his paws on Mia's knees. "Mia, you could use your magic to look back into the past at the shelters being destroyed and the campfire being put out and see what happened."

"Okay."

Mia got out her mirror. Cupping it in her hands, she tried to clear her mind so that she could connect with the magic current, but her thoughts were churning—the fire, the shelters, the boots. She frowned as the surface of the mirror stayed stubbornly mirror-like.

Bracken leaned against her. "Try to relax. Remember, you can't connect to the current if your mind is too busy. Pet me."

Mia smoothed his soft fur and breathed deeply. Her thoughts began to clear, and this time, the current tingled and sparked through her, and the mirror swirled.

She saw a small, shadowy figure darting between the shelters. Mia frowned. It seemed to be moving on four legs, and was that a long, furry tail? Branches flew across the glade until the movement suddenly stopped, and all that was left were the damaged and destroyed shelters. The image changed to the campfire. She saw the barrels being tipped over one after the other and then, just for the briefest of moments, she glimpsed a small face with dark eyes and fluffy ears. A memory stirred in her mind, but then it was gone.

Mia lowered the mirror and told the others what she had seen.

"It sounds like a Shade," said Bracken. "They move really fast."

"But we couldn't smell any Shades yesterday when we looked around," said Willow.

"Maybe that's because it wasn't here yesterday," suggested Violet.

Sorrel nodded.

Mia picked up her mirror again. She'd had an idea. *Show me if a Shade is doing all these things here at camp*, she thought.

The mirror swirled but no picture appeared.

"What can you see?" Bracken asked.

"Nothing. But there could be some kind of blocking spell."

People using dark magic could perform such spells so that they couldn't be spied on.

Mia frowned. "Though usually…." She shook her head and broke off. Usually she saw a dark cloud, not just nothing like this, but maybe that wasn't important. She decided not to mention it. "No, it doesn't matter. It must be a blocking spell."

"If there is a Shade, who conjured it?" Lexi said.

"And why? Who'd want to cause trouble

here in camp?" said Sita.

"I know!" Violet exclaimed. "Mrs. Coates!"

Mia caught her breath. Of course! The bad-tempered farmer wanted the camp to fail. She had a reason for ruining things. Mia grabbed her mirror. "Show me Mrs. Coates with anything magical!"

A picture immediately appeared of Mrs. Coates on the porch of her house with a bag over one shoulder. There were house plants on shelves and rain boots by the door. Mia saw her march off the porch and get into her truck.

"It *is* Mrs. Coates!" Mia exclaimed.

"Did you see what object the Shade is trapped in?" Bracken asked eagerly.

"No. But it could have been in the bag she was carrying," said Mia.

Sorrel paced around the tent. "We need to find out what that object is – and where it is."

Juniper leaped onto Lexi's head. "But how?"

They heard the drum banging. "It's dinnertime," said Sita.

"Let's think up a plan at bedtime," said Mia.

They all nodded.

Mia jumped to her feet, feeling a rush of determination. Wherever the Shade was, whatever it was hidden in, they would find it and stop it before it did anything else!

As they made their way to the campfire, Lexi whispered to the others, "Are we still going to prank the boys into thinking mice have been in their tent?"

"We might as well," said Mia.

Lexi grinned. "Cool! I'll get some rice from

the storage room."

The pizza was delicious. While everyone was cleaning up, Lexi pulled the others to one side. She had slipped into the storage room and her pockets were now bulging with rice.

"Sita, can you and Violet make sure the boys don't come back to their tent?" she whispered. "Mia and I will set the prank up."

Lexi and Mia ran to the boys' tent and scattered the wild black rice across their sleeping bags and up onto the crate, where they were keeping their midnight snacks. It looked just like mouse droppings!

"Final touches," said Lexi, picking up a chocolate bar and nibbling at the wrapper with her teeth.

Mia giggled. It looked like an army of mice had been having a party in the tent!

Lexi placed a few grains of rice near a cuddly animal on one of the beds. "All done."

"Wait!"

Mia's attention was caught by the toy. It was a fluffy raccoon. Another raccoon popped into her head—a pottery raccoon with a long tail, large eyes in a mask-like face, and little front paws—paws that would make prints that looked almost like tiny human hands....

She gasped. "Lexi, I think I know what Mrs. Coates has trapped the Shade in!"

9
POTTERY AND
PRANKS

Mia and Lexi raced out of the tent. They
charged over to the others, who were hovering
near the edges of the campfire. Everyone else
was starting to sit down and get ready to toast
marshmallows. Mia beckoned Violet and Sita
over and pulled them into a huddle, then she
told them what she'd just figured out.

"The pottery raccoon?" Violet whispered,
her eyes wide. "You think Mrs. Coates trapped
the Shade in that?"

Mia nodded. "It fits! I had a dream where

I saw an animal with little hands and big round eyes following me through the forest. And I saw some strange tracks near our tent and by the shelters. I think they could have been made by the raccoon."

"So the Shade stole our boots?" said Sita. "As well as destroyed the shelters and putting out the fire?"

Mia nodded.

Lexi frowned. "But why? How would stealing our boots wreck the camp?"

"I don't know," Mia said impatiently. "Maybe it was going to steal everyone's boots, but it got disturbed. It's the raccoon. I'm sure it is! Mrs. Coates is the only person who wants the camp to fail, and the bad things all started happening *after* she left the raccoon here."

"Hang on," said Violet suddenly. "Mrs. Coates told us she'd found the raccoon on her porch. She said it wasn't hers."

"She must have been lying," Mia said.

"Pretending so she had an excuse to leave the raccoon here."

They all nodded.

"We need to find that raccoon," said Violet.

"Miss Amadi said she was going to keep it," said Mia. "It's probably in her tent."

"Then let's get it while she's at the campfire with the others!" said Violet.

"Wait! We'll get into a ton of trouble if someone sees us going into Miss Amadi's tent," said Sita.

Violet grinned. "Then let's not be seen. We can shadow-travel in!"

When Violet connected to the magic current, she could move from place to place by moving through shadows, and she could take the others with her if she were holding their hands.

"Mia, why don't you come with me? Lexi, Sita, you keep watch. If Miss Amadi gets up from the campfire and looks like she's heading for her tent, then distract her."

"Okay!" Lexi and Sita agreed.

Violet turned to Mia, her eyes shining. "Are you ready for some fun!"

"Definitely!" Mia replied.

They ran into the nearby trees where the shadows were dark. Violet took Mia's hand. "Here we go!"

She shut her eyes, and suddenly, Mia felt as if the world were falling away. She had the sensation of spinning around very quickly in space, and then her feet bumped into the ground.

Her eyes blinked open. They were in Miss Amadi's tent, and it was very dark. She could just make out the glow of the solar-powered lanterns on the ground outside.

"Flashlights!" Violet hissed.

They pulled them out of their pockets and switched them on. The teacher's tent looked just as it had before, the giraffe throw pulled over the bed, ornaments and trinkets neatly arranged on top of the upside-down crates. Mia shined her flashlight over them, her gaze darting across the ornaments—a brass elephant, a bowl of crystals, the carved monkey Miss Amadi had been silly with, a silver otter, several necklaces and rings, and the stuffed toy sloth. However, there was no sign of the pottery raccoon with the pink crystal in its hands.

Violet searched behind the crates, and Mia looked under the throw on the bed and shined the flashlight around the edges of the tent.

"It's not here," Violet whispered.

Suddenly, there was a loud yell outside the tent.

"Ow! Ouch! Ow!" they heard Lexi shouting dramatically. "My ankle!"

"Oh, my goodness, Lexi, are you okay?" came Miss Amadi's voice.

"Miss Amadi!" Mia hissed. "We've got to get out of here!"

Violet grabbed her hand, and Mia felt the magic carrying them away. They stepped out of the shadows in the trees just in time to see the other campers heading off to their tents for the night. Lexi and Sita were with Miss Amadi. Sita spotted Violet and Mia and nudged Lexi. Immediately, Lexi's hobbling grew less.

"Oh, it's getting better," she said to Miss Amadi.

"Are you sure you don't need me to wrap it up?" Miss Amadi said in concern.

"No thanks—I'll be alright," said Lexi. "I must have just twisted it."

Mia and Violet hurried over. "Are you okay, Lexi?" Violet asked innocently.

"Yes, I'm fine," said Lexi, hiding her grin.

Just then, there was a yell from Dan, Nikhil, and Josh's tent, and the three boys came scrambling out. "Miss Amadi! We have mice in our tent!" exclaimed Dan, seeing Miss Amadi.

"They pooped on all our things!" said Nikhil.

Miss Amadi sighed. "Let me take a look." She shone her torch in through the flap. "Oh, dear." She ducked inside and then they heard her start to chuckle. "Boys, I don't think you've got mice," she said as she came out, smiling.

"What?" Dan said. "But there's mouse poop everywhere."

"Ha! Pranked you!" said Mia, high-fiving Lexi.

"It's not poop—it's just rice," said Lexi, giggling.

"What?" exclaimed Josh.

"Got you!" said Lexi.

The boys ran back into the tent. "It *is* rice," they heard Nikhil say.

The boys came out, laughing. Miss Amadi joined in.

"Good trick, girls. Okay, everyone, time for bed now."

Grinning at each other, the girls went into their tent.

Once camp was quiet, Sorrel and Willow
went to see if they could sniff out the Shade.
Meanwhile, Mia tried her magic again. She
knew it wouldn't show her the Shade, but
she'd thought of something else she could try.
Holding the mirror, she whispered, "Please
show me where the raccoon ornament is."

The mirror swirled, and she saw plants—some
with wide, glossy green leaves and others with
long, narrow leaves with green and white stripes.

"I can see plants," Mia said. "It must be
hiding in the forest." She frowned as she
studied the picture. Something about the plants
didn't look quite right….

Sorrel and Willow came back into the tent.
Mia lowered the mirror.

"Did you find the Shade?" Violet asked.

"No," said Sorrel. "We couldn't smell it at all."

"The magic's just showed me that it's in the

forest," said Mia. "It might be too far away for you to smell."

"Or it might not be a Shade," Willow said.

"It has to be," said Mia. "I saw it moving really fast like Shades do, and it's making horrible things happen."

"Causing chaos and trouble," said Juniper, nodding. "Just like a Shade."

Sorrel flexed her claws. "I think we animals should watch over the campsite tonight. If it tries anything, we'll wake you."

"And then we'll catch it!" Violet exclaimed.

Mia nodded determinedly. "And save the camp!"

10
Monkey Mischief

That night, Mia dreamed she was in the forest. She was being followed by something. The leaves were rustling, and she could see a shadowy shape jumping from branch to branch in the trees. Her heart sped up. What did it want? Why was it following her? She started to run but tripped on a tree root. As she lay sprawled on the ground, she looked up and saw a little face with dark markings around its eyes and round ears peering at her through the thick green leaves....

Mia woke up. She could hear birds outside and could tell from the light that the sun was rising. She sat up in bed and saw Bracken lying by the tent entrance, his head poking out under the flap.

"Bracken!" she whispered.

He pulled his head back in and took a running leap on to the bed. She cuddled him. "Is everything okay?"

"Yes," he said. "The campsite's been quiet all night.

Juniper went out earlier and checked the shelters, and they haven't been touched."

Mia felt a rush of relief. "Phew!"

"What activities do you have today?"
Bracken asked.

"A treasure hunt this morning," said Mia,
remembering what Connie had told them the
night before. "Then this evening we're having a
quiz competition. Oh, and this afternoon, we're
going to a river outside the camp to swim and
climb the rocks."

"I really don't want to do that!" said Violet,
waking up and overhearing. "What if the Shade
decides to try and hurt someone while they're
climbing?"

The thought had crossed Mia's mind, too.
It would be the perfect opportunity for the
Shade. "We'll stay alert," she said.

They got dressed, said good-bye to their
animals, and went to have breakfast. Mia
pushed the oatmeal around in her bowl. She
didn't feel hungry, even though they hadn't
eaten their midnight snack the night before.
None of them had felt like it—they'd been too

worried about the Shade.

After breakfast, each team was given a map and a list of clues, which—if solved—would lead them to their own box of treasure.

Mia and her friends set off into the trees. The chatter of the other groups faded until they were just left with the sound of birds singing and the crunch of their feet on pine needles. A butterfly fluttered past Mia's nose. If she hadn't been feeling so on edge, she would have really been enjoying going on a treasure hunt in the forest, but as they went deeper into the trees, her feeling of foreboding grew.

Violet and Lexi led the way, reading out the clues. Mia didn't really pay attention—she was too busy scanning the treetops. Maybe it was because of her dream the night before, but she had the distinct feeling they were being spied on. Overhead, a tree branch shook. She glanced up and gasped as she caught a glimpse of something jumping through the air.

"What's up?" said Violet, looking around.

"There's something in the trees," Mia said. "I think it's following us."

"I'll go and check," said Lexi.

She took a deep breath, connecting with the current, and then began to climb a nearby tree. Using the magic, she was as agile as a squirrel. They watched as she got higher and higher before coming to rest on a branch and looking all around. She shook her head at them, then swiftly climbed down.

"I couldn't see anything."

Mia bit her lip. "I'm sure the raccoon is up there somewhere. I think we should call the animals. They can vanish if anyone comes. Bracken!"

The others joined in. "Juniper!"

"Sorrel!"

"Willow!"

The animals were there in a second.

"Has something happened?" Sorrel asked Violet.

"Not yet, but Mia thinks we're being followed," she replied.

"I went into the trees, but I couldn't see anything," said Lexi.

"Let's keep going," said Mia. "But be careful!"

They set off again with the animals at their sides. Every rustle made them jump and look around. Mia was very glad she had Bracken there. She had just paused to pet him when an acorn fell from above, almost hitting her. Glancing up, she saw a face peering at her from between some leaves.

"There!" she cried, pointing.

The face vanished. Mia saw the leaves rustling ahead of them and knew the raccoon must be leaping from branch to branch. She set off deeper into the trees after it.

"It's going that way! Come on!" she shouted.

They all charged after her, jumping over roots and rabbit holes. As they ran, Mia felt something niggling at the back of her mind. The creature's face hadn't looked quite right, but she couldn't figure out why.

"We've gone past the boundary of the camp!" Sita exclaimed.

"Who cares?" panted Violet. "We have to catch it!"

"I'm faster than any of you if I use magic," said Lexi. "I'll get it!"

"No! Wait!" said Sita. "I know what to do!"

She stopped and shouted up into the trees. "Spirit, I command you to come down!"

"Great idea, Sita," breathed Mia as the trees stopped rustling.

"Get ready to grab it and send it back to the shadows," said Sorrel.

They waited with bated breath as a small creature with a long tail emerged from the tree canopy and began to climb down the tree trunk.

Something wasn't right. Mia realized it instantly. The animal had a plain tail, not a striped one like a raccoon, and its body was a different shape. It stopped at the base of the trunk and turned around to look at them. As Mia saw its face, she felt a lurch of shock. It was the monkey from Miss Amadi's tent!

"That's not the raccoon!" said Violet in astonishment.

"It might not be, but the Shade's inside it!" Mia cried, leaping toward the monkey. The others followed her. "Come here, you … ahhh!" Mia shrieked as the ground suddenly gave way beneath her feet. The branches they had just run over had been disguising a deep pit!

They tumbled into it, their arms flailing, before they landed on a pile of leaves and heather.

"Mia, are you okay?" asked Bracken, jumping up and licking her face.

"Yes, I'm fine," she said, sitting up and feeling

relieved when she saw the others sitting up, too. Lexi was rubbing her head as if she'd banged it, but everyone else looked uninjured.

The monkey peered over the edge of the pit and smiled broadly. "Good!" it said, sounding very pleased with itself. "My plan worked. Now you won't have to go rock climbing."

Mia felt a rush of confusion. *Rock climbing?*

"What are you talking about, you silly creature?" hissed Sorrel. "And why have you put us in this … this dirty hole!" Her whiskers quivered with outrage.

"Temper, temper! I'm just doing what I was told and making sure that *she*—" the monkey pointed at Violet—"has a good time at camp."

"What do you mean?" Mia demanded.

"That was the instruction I was given when Star Magic woke me up and I've been carrying it out ever since," the monkey said. "And doing very well, if I do say so myself. I've been popping out of Ginni's tent whenever I've been needed. I helped Violet find the things she wanted on the scavenger hunt, I got rid of her boots so she wouldn't have to climb trees, I destroyed the structure so she wouldn't have to sleep in it, and I put out the fire so she wouldn't have to cook on it." It turned a somersault. "I've been a very helpful monkey!"

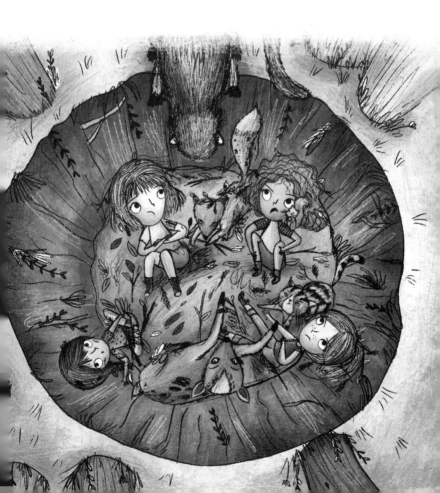

Mia stared at it. "You mean, everything that's happened was because of Violet?"

"And it wasn't Mrs. Coates trying to sabotage the camp?" Lexi burst out.

"Mrs. Coates?" said the monkey, looking puzzled. "Who's she?"

Mia could hardly believe it. They'd gotten it so wrong!

"Hang on," Violet said suddenly. "What do you mean, Star Magic woke you up?"

The monkey looked surprised. "You should know—you were there. When I felt the touch of Star Magic, I woke up and heard the instruction to make sure you had a good time. That's what I've been doing ever since."

"I don't understand this. Are you some kind of Wish Shade?" asked Sita.

The monkey slapped its legs and chuckled. "Me? A Wish Shade? Oh, no!"

Violet stared the little animal straight in the eyes. "Well, whatever kind of Shade you are, I am a Spirit Speaker with the power to command spirits to return to their own worlds. I command you to return to the shadows where you belong!"

They waited for the Shade to shriek in annoyance and spiral out of the monkey, but nothing happened.

"Why is it not going back to the shadows?" Violet asked Sorrel.

"Because it's not a Shade," said Sorrel, her indigo gaze fixed on the monkey who was chuckling to itself. "It is a different kind of spirit altogether."

"The Star Cat is correct. I am a Jeniyan Spirit from the Realm of Light," said the monkey, waggling its ears. "A good spirit who helps people." It gave them a mischievous grin.

"Oh, no," groaned Bracken, covering his muzzle with his front paws. "I've heard of good spirits like this. They can cause just as much trouble as Shades. They might not mean

to, but they do."

"I don't cause trouble," the monkey said indignantly. "I help people!"

"Do you think you could help us out of this pit?" said Violet hopefully.

The monkey shook its head and backed away. "Oh, no, no, no. If I did that, you would have to go rock climbing and you might also eat the poisoned candy."

"The *what*?" Mia said, feeling her stomach drop.

"Poisoned candy?" echoed Sita.

"Yes, I'm off to poison the candy in those treasure boxes!" said the monkey cheerily.

"But why?" gasped Mia.

"So that everyone who eats them will get sick, then they won't be able to take part in the quiz competition and Violet will win. I know she likes to win things." The monkey beamed.

They all spoke at once.

"No! Don't!"

"You can't poison people!"

"I don't want to win that much!" Violet cried.

"Don't worry!" The monkey turned another somersault. "The plant poison I'm using will just make the other campers very sick for a night. The adults will be fine as long as they don't eat the candy, which means they'll still be able to run the competition so you can win. I'll be back once I've gotten to all of the treasure boxes!" It waved its tail at them.

"*Byeeee!*"

"Wait! I command you to stop!" cried Sita.

The monkey had its fingers in its ears and was singing loudly. "*La-la-la-la-la!* Can't hear you, Commanding One!"

"We've got to do something!" Mia cried. "Lexi, can you get out of this pit?"

"I'm feeling a bit dizzy," admitted Lexi. "I bumped my head when we fell in here." She looked up to where a tree root was sticking out of the pit wall. "But if Sita could heal me, and someone could give me a boost, then I could try and reach that root and then…."

"It's escaping! There isn't time!" said Violet as the monkey jumped away from the edge of the pit. "Quick! Mia, hold this for me!" She grabbed a large fir branch off the floor of the pit and held it up like an umbrella.

"What? Why?" said Mia, taking it.

"We have to stop that monkey right now!" said Violet. And jumping into the small patch of shadow under the fir branch, she vanished!

11
AMAZING VIOLET

There was a moment of stunned silence in
the pit and then Sorrel vanished, too, and they
heard Violet shouting. "You stop right there,
monkey! You're not going to ruin camp for
everyone! You are not to put poisoned candy
in the treasure boxes!"

Mia pulled the mirror out of her pocket.
"Show me what Violet's doing!"

A picture appeared, and Mia watched
intently.

"The monkey's scrambling up a tree," she

told the others. "Oh my goodness, Violet's going after it!"

"But she's scared of heights!" Lexi burst out.

"I guess she knows she won't be able to command it to return to its own world unless she's looking into its eyes," Mia said. "Sorrel's with her. They're both climbing the tree."

"Sita, can you use your magic to stop me from feeling dizzy?" said Lexi. "I need to help them!"

Sita nodded. She put her hand gently on Lexi's head and connected with the current as Mia continued to describe what she could see as she watched Sorrel overtake Violet and claw her way up the oak tree, determination on her tabby face. The monkey started to talk, and Mia lifted the mirror closer to her so she could hear what it was saying.

"I thought you didn't like climbing trees, Violet, but it's fun, isn't it?" she heard the monkey say gleefully as Violet edged up the tree.

Mia saw Sorrel veering off along a branch underneath the monkey. The cat crawled across it, and then her muscles tensed and she leaped through the air, landing on the next tree, her sharp claws digging into the trunk to stop herself from falling.

The monkey was too busy watching Violet to notice her. "You're almost up as high as me now,

Violet!" it said encouragingly. "I'm glad you've finally realized how much fun climbing is!"

"I am not climbing for fun! I'm going to get you, and I'm going to stop you!" Violet panted as she hauled herself onto a thick branch that was level with it.

"Ow," she winced as an overhanging branch scratched her cheek. Ignoring the scratch, she struggled farther along the branch until she was sitting astride it, her back to the trunk, her legs wrapped around the branch.

"Shall we play tag now that you're up

here?" cried the monkey. It turned to swing away and then shrieked in shock as it came face-to-face with a very angry Sorrel, who had snuck up behind it. She swiped at it with her paw and it leaped backward, falling right into Violet's arms.

"Got you!" Violet exclaimed, wobbling precariously as she held it by the scruff of its neck. The monkey struggled, but she hung on grimly and looked it straight in the eyes. "Jeniyan Spirit, I command you to return to the Realm of Light!"

For a moment, the monkey's eyes sparkled incredibly brightly, and then they dulled as the spirit returned to its own realm and it became just a plain wooden ornament again.

Mia saw the relief cross Violet's face. She sagged back against the trunk but then glanced down and seemed to realize how high up she was. The relief on her face turned to fear, and she clung to the tree trunk. She looked too scared to move, and the scratch on her face was bleeding.

"Violet sent the spirit back to its own world," Mia said in alarm. "But now she's stuck in the tree! She looks terrified."

Juniper leaped around anxiously. "We need to help her get down, Lexi. Are you feeling better now?"

"I'm completely back to normal," said Lexi, throwing a smile at Sita. "Thanks, Sita!"

"No problem," said Sita. "Do you think you can help Violet?"

Lexi jumped to her feet. "I'm sure I can. Mia, can you give me a boost?"

"Sure." Mia cupped her hands together.

Lexi took a deep breath, connecting to the current, and then she stepped onto Mia's hands and sprang lightly upward, her hands grabbing for the tree root that was sticking out of the pit wall above their heads. She swung from it for a moment, built up momentum, and then somersaulted effortlessly out of the pit. Juniper vanished and reappeared beside her at the top.

"Good luck!" called Mia.

"Get Violet down safely!" begged Sita.

Mia used the mirror to watch as Lexi nimbly climbed the tree Violet was in. Sorrel had edged along the branch until she was beside her Star Friend.

"It will be all right," she was saying. "Lexi and Juniper are coming." Her usually sharp voice was soothing. Violet let go of the branch with one trembling hand and petted her.

"I'm glad you're here with me, Sorrel," she said shakily.

"You are incredible," Sorrel told her. "So brave. You stopped the monkey from poisoning everyone, and now you just need to stay brave so you can get down the tree. Lexi and Juniper are going to help. No, don't look at the ground," she said firmly. "Just keep looking at me."

Violet nodded and continued to pet her, her eyes fixed on Sorrel's indigo ones.

Mia saw Lexi and Juniper reach them. "Okay, I'm going to guide your feet down,"

Lexi said. "Put your weight where I say."

"I'll guide your hands," said Juniper.

"And I'm here right beside you," said Sorrel. She rubbed her head against Violet's cheek. "You can do this, Violet."

Violet took a deep breath and nodded.

Little by little, Lexi, Juniper, and Sorrel helped her down the tree until her feet were finally back on solid ground.

Mia hugged Sita. "She's safe!" she exclaimed as Violet sagged against the trunk. She turned back to the mirror.

"That was really scary!" Violet said.

"But you did it," said Lexi, hugging her. "You were so brave going up there after the monkey, especially when you're scared of heights."

Sorrel rubbed her head against Violet's arm, purring proudly.

"There was no way I was going to let it poison people," said Violet. She put a hand to her bleeding cheek. "Ow."

"We need to get Mia and Sita out of the pit," said Lexi.

"Please do!" Mia shouted up to them.

"Do you think we can make a rope from creepers?" Lexi asked Violet.

"No need." Violet straightened up. The next moment, Mia and Sita saw her look over the edge of the pit. "Get that fir branch ready to make some shadows, Mia," she grinned, looking much more like her normal self. "I'm coming in!"

In next to no time, Violet had shadow-traveled into the pit and shadow-traveled them back out. At the top, they all hugged, the animals leaping around them in delight. Sita used her magic to heal Violet's wound, the deep scratch fading to a pink line and then vanishing completely.

"You were awesome!" Mia told Violet.

"So brave!" said Sita.

Violet pushed her hands through her hair.

"I just couldn't let the monkey ruin camp for everyone." She picked up the carved wooden ornament from the ground and shook her head. "I can't believe all the things that have happened were because a spirit was trying to make sure I had a good time!"

"Do you think Miss Amadi knew the monkey had a Jeniyan Spirit in it?" said Lexi.

"No," said Violet. "Remember it said it was woken up by the touch of Star Magic. I must have done it by accident."

"But when did you touch it?' Lexi asked.

"Miss Amadi put it into my hands," said Violet. "And told it to make sure I had a good time at camp."

Mia frowned. She thought Miss Amadi had said that and *then* put the monkey in Violet's hands. *I'm probably remembering it wrong*, she thought.

Sita smiled. "Can you imagine how surprised Miss Amadi would be if she realized she'd started something magical?"

"You don't think there's a chance she knew about the magic, do you?" Mia said slowly.

"Definitely not," said Violet immediately. "She seemed just as shocked as everyone else when the structures were destroyed and the campfire put out."

"And when our boots went missing," added Lexi.

"If she'd known the monkey was doing those things, I'm sure she'd have tried to stop it," said Sita.

Mia nodded. They were right. And anyway Miss Amadi couldn't have woken up the spirit— it had been Star Magic that had done that.

"We'd better put it back before she notices it's missing," said Violet.

"Okay, but first, let's fill the pit in," said Mia. "We don't want anyone else to fall in it!"

They piled soil and branches into the hole and started back to camp.

"We haven't found our team's treasure," Lexi remembered as they walked back along the forest path.

Mia pulled out her mirror. "Cheating might be allowed just this once!"

Using the magic, she found that their treasure box was hidden near the structures. They retrieved it, then hurried back to camp. The animals vanished as they got close.

"Goodness, what happened to you?" Miss Amadi said, looking at their muddy hands and dirt-smudged faces.

"And what took you so long? We were just about to send out a search party!" said Connie.

"We … um … fell," said Mia.

"And got a little muddy," said Lexi.

Connie laughed. "You certainly did. Well, never mind. You can wash it off in the river this afternoon!"

It was wonderful playing in the river, knowing they'd stopped the Jeniyan Spirit from ruining camp. They swam and splashed in the clear water and then climbed the rocks behind the river, although Violet stayed on solid ground.

"I am definitely done with climbing today," she told them, sitting on her towel and wriggling her toes in the sun.

The campfire that night was the best yet. They had to pair up with another tent for the quiz about the forest. Mia and the others formed a team with Alyssa, Hannah, Anoushka, and Maddie. It was fun being with the other girls, and Mia was happy to see that Maddie seemed to have made friends with the rest of her tent. Violet and Lexi answered almost all of the questions, but Maddie knew a lot about animals, and she was the one who answered the tie-breaking question to win first prize for her team.

"What is the name for an otter's home?" Miss Amadi asked.

Maddie's hand shot up. "A holt!"

Miss Amadi smiled. "Correct! I declare your team the winners!"

Their prizes were two huge bars of chocolate and badges in the shape of trees to put on their backpacks.

After the competition, they had burgers and hot dogs with lots of ketchup and big bowls of salad.

"This has been a wonderful vacation," said Mia happily as she licked her fingers.

"The best!" agreed Lexi.

"We've done so many fun things," said Sita.

Mia nudged Violet. "So you're glad you didn't go home, then?"

Violet grinned. "Very! It's been awesome!"

Miss Amadi was passing by and overheard. "I said you'd have a great time."

The girls exchanged looks. If only she knew!

After the plates had been cleaned up, Connie melted chocolate in a pan over the fire while the rest of the guides handed out strawberries, marshmallows, and sticks.

Mia was just making up her second skewer to dip into the melted chocolate when a car drove into the parking lot and Mrs. Coates came walking over to the campfire. Mia's heart sank. They were having so much fun. The last thing they needed was Mrs. Coates being grumpy.

"Mrs. Coates," Connie said nervously. "Can I help you?"

To everyone's astonishment, the gray-haired

farmer smiled. "Actually, I thought I might be able to help you. I've brought some fresh eggs for your breakfast tomorrow. They're in my truck."

"Oh." Connie looked completely taken aback. "Wow, that's very kind of you."

"One good turn deserves another. It was very good of your campers to make those toys and food garlands for my chickens," said Mrs. Coates.

"No problem. If it's useful, we can make them as a regular part of the camp program," said Connie. "Using up food is much better than throwing it away."

Mrs. Coates looked happy. "Thank you. And, if you'd like the campers to see the farm, I'm happy to show them around—and provide you with eggs."

"This is weird. Why's she being so nice?" Mia whispered to Violet.

"Because of the chicken toys we made—like she said?" suggested Violet, losing interest in Mrs. Coates and turning away to talk to Lexi.

Mia frowned. Making the toys had been a nice idea, but was it really enough to have changed Mrs. Coates's attitude so dramatically?

Miss Amadi brought a plate of strawberries and marshmallows over to Mrs Coates. "Why don't you join us? It's great when neighbors take part."

"You're right, my dear," said Mrs. Coates. "And I have to say that ever since you dropped those toys and that raccoon ornament off, I've been feeling differently about this camp."

Mia stiffened. *Raccoon!* They'd been so busy dealing with the monkey that she'd forgotten about the raccoon. Had Miss Amadi given him back to Mrs. Coates, then?

"I've decided to keep him on my porch with my potted plants," Mrs. Coates went on.

Mia's eyes widened as she suddenly realized why the plants she'd seen with the raccoon had seemed odd—they were tropical plants, not plants you'd get in the forest.

"I still have no idea who left him at my house in the first place," the farmer went on, "but I'm glad you brought him back." She shook her head. "He's a funny little thing with his big pink acorn, but I do like him."

"I'm so happy to hear that," Miss Amadi said. "I was going to keep him, but I thought about what it said on the acorn and decided that the right thing to do was to give him back to you as a gift of friendship. I'm glad you accepted him."

"I wonder where he came from," said Mrs. Coates.

"I guess we'll never know," Miss Amadi

said. She clapped her hands to get everyone's attention. "Okay, I think it's time for a sing-along!"

As Mrs. Coates sat down, Mia frowned. She still didn't think that the chicken toys could make that much of a difference in Mrs. Coates' attitude. Could there be magic at work?

Jacob started playing his guitar, and Sita slipped her arm through Mia's. "I feel so happy."

"Me, too." Mia gave up puzzling about Mrs. Coates. Maybe the farmer's change of heart was due to magic, maybe it wasn't. *The important thing is that she seems to have stopped wanting to shut the camp down,* Mia decided.

Violet stretched. "I can definitely say this is the best camping trip I've ever been on."

Lexi chuckled. "It's the only camping trip you've ever been on."

"Yep, and it's definitely the best!" Violet said with a grin.

Mia looked at her friends. "You know what I

think would make things even better, though?"

"Getting to finally eat our midnight snack tonight?" Lexi said.

"Well, yes, that, of course," said Mia. "But I think it would be better right now if we were somewhere that no one could see us." She glanced pointedly at the trees behind them and saw understanding dawning on the others' faces.

Getting up, they all slipped away from the campfire. A few minutes later, they were sitting in their own circle with their animals cuddled beside them.

Gazing at the stars twinkling above them and listening to the music and chatter coming from the campfire, Mia felt a warm rush of happiness. She might not have solved every single mystery at camp, but they'd solved most of them, and they'd had an amazing time. *A magical time*, she thought, bending down to kiss Bracken's fluffy head. He gave a contented sigh and snuggled even closer into her arms.

Enchanted Mist

Turn the page for
a sneak peek of
the Star Friends
next adventure!

Coming soon...

In the Star World

A snowy owl with silver feathers swooped silently through the forest and came to land on the edge of a rocky pool with a mirror-like surface. The branches of the tall trees around the pool reached up to the star-filled sky, their leaves and trunks glittering. There was a faint rustle as three more animals appeared out of the shadows—a stag, a wolf, and a badger. Their fur was tipped with silver, and their expressions were wise.

"It appears our four young Star Animals and their Star Friends from Westport have managed to stop magic from causing chaos again," said Hunter the owl, sweeping one wing over the pool. An image of a campfire surrounded by children and adults appeared on the surface.

A little way off, nestled against some trees, four girls were cuddling four animals—a young fox, a fallow deer, a red squirrel, and a wildcat with a tabby coat. The animals all had indigo eyes just like the wolf, the stag, the badger, and the owl. Everyone looked very happy.

"They did well," the wolf said softly. "It helps that they have such a strong friendship."

The others nodded.

"They worked together and kept people from getting hurt," said the stag.

"But they haven't yet realized that there is another Star Animal close by," said Hunter.

The picture changed to show a sleek brown otter with sparkling indigo eyes.

"Fen is inexperienced with Star Magic and needs to learn more. Her Star Friend must also learn not to use other forms of magic unwisely.

I hope our young friends will be able to help."

"They need to find Fen first," said the badger.

"Let's hope they do before the magic causes more problems," said the stag.

"Shall we see what happens when they return to Westport?" said the wolf.

The others nodded, and they all settled down to watch.

COLLECT THEM ALL!

Star Friends
NIGHT SHADOWS

BY LINDA CHAPMAN
ILLUSTRATED BY LUCY FLEMING
5

Star Friends
POISON POTION

BY LINDA CHAPMAN
ILLUSTRATED BY LUCY FLEMING
6

Star Friends
MOONLIGHT MISCHIEF

BY LINDA CHAPMAN
ILLUSTRATED BY LUCY FLEMING
7

Star Friends
HIDDEN CHARM

BY LINDA CHAPMAN
ILLUSTRATED BY LUCY FLEMING
8

MORE FROM LINDA:

MERMAIDS ROCK

The Coral Kingdom

by Linda Chapman

Illustrated by
Mirelle Ortega

1

Marina is new in Mermaids Rock. She has travelled the world with her scientist dad, and she can't wait to make friends! She meets a group of mermaids who love animals and the environment as much as she does and the new friends soon face their first challenge.... The beautiful coral caves nearby have been damaged. Who, or what, could have caused the destruction? And why?

mermaids ROCK

The Floating Forest

by Linda Chapman

Illustrated by
Mirelle Ortega

Coralie is overjoyed when she visits a beautiful kelp forest, where she meets adorable sea lions and otters and finds a mysterious treasure map! After telling her friends about it, they're excited to search for the treasure, but when they arrive they find the forest has been destroyed. With no protection from the plants, the animals are in danger, and the friends must do everything they can to save the creatures before it's too late....

MORE FROM LINDA:

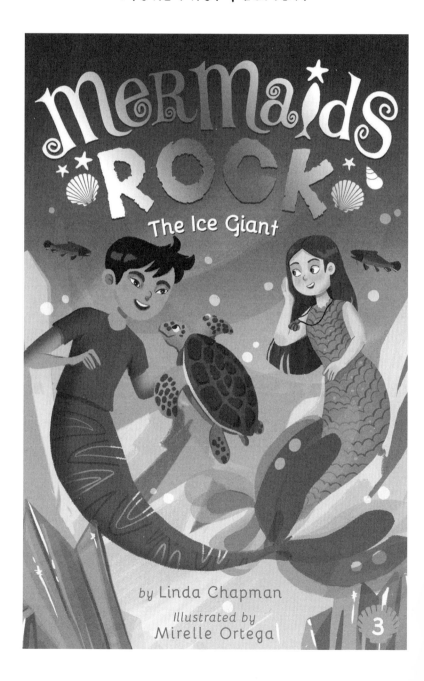

MERMAIDS ROCK

The Ice Giant

by Linda Chapman

Illustrated by
Mirelle Ortega

3

Kai is really excited that Marina is coming to stay while her dad goes on a research trip to the Arctic–they're going to have so much fun! But when they don't hear from him for a few days they start to worry. Travelling through the whirlpool to see if they can find him, the friends are amazed by the icy scene and enchanted by the walruses they meet. But with no sign of Marina's dad and time running out, can the team work together to save the day?

ABOUT THE AUTHOR

Linda Chapman is the best-selling author of more than 200 books. The biggest compliment she can have is for a child to tell her he or she became a reader after reading one of her books. She lives in a cottage with a tower in Leicestershire, England, with her husband, three children, three dogs, and three ponies. When she's not writing, Linda likes to ride, read, and visit schools and libraries to talk to people about writing.

ABOUT THE ILLUSTRATOR

Kim Barnes lives on the Isle of Wight with her partner and two children, Leo and Cameo, who greatly inspire her work. She graduated from Lincoln University, England, and has drawn ever since she was a young child.

www.kimmariaillustration.com